❖ The Boy ❖
Who Cried Wolf

❖ The Boy ❖
Who Cried Wolf

TONY ROSS

Dial Books for Young Readers

New York

a pied piper book

For Zöe and Katy

First published in the United States 1985 by
Dial Books for Young Readers
A Division of Penguin Books USA Inc.
375 Hudson Street
New York, New York 10014

Published in Great Britain by Andersen Press
Copyright © 1985 by Tony Ross
All rights reserved
Library of Congress Catalog Card Number: 84-23273
Printed in Hong Kong
First Pied Piper Printing 1991
E
1 3 5 7 9 10 8 6 4 2

A Pied Piper Book is a registered trademark of
Dial Books for Young Readers,
a division of Penguin Books USA Inc.,
® TM 1,163,686 and ® TM 1,054,312.

THE BOY WHO CRIED WOLF
is published in a hardcover edition by
Dial Books for Young Readers.
ISBN 0-8037-0911-0

The art for each picture consists of a black ink
and watercolor painting, which is scanner-separated
and reproduced in full color.

Once upon a time a little boy lived on this side
of the mountains. His name was Willy.

On the other side of the mountains a wolf lived
in the lap of luxury. Nobody ever asked *his* name.

The wolf had fine manners (for a wolf).
Sometimes he put on his dinner jacket...

and came over the mountains
...for dinner.

Because the wolf liked dining on people, everybody on this side of the mountains was afraid of him.
So...

whenever Willy had to do something he didn't
want to, like take a bath,

he would cry "wolf" (even if the wolf was nowhere
to be seen).
Because everybody was afraid of the wolf...

Willy was left alone to do just what he wanted.

Once a week Willy went for his violin lesson.
Because he hated his lessons...

he cried "wolf," even though the wolf was not around.

Then Willy was left alone to play the kind of music *he* liked.

Sometimes Willy even cried "wolf"
just for the fun of it.

One day Willy was riding in the mountains
when the wolf jumped out from the rocks.

"WOLF!" cried Willy.
He ran back to town crying "WOLF, WOLF"
all the way.

"WOLF!" cried Willy, but his grandmother didn't
believe him. Willy always cried "wolf."
"Tell me another one!" she said.

"WOLF" cried Willy, but nobody listened.

"Save me from the WOLF!" shrieked Willy,
but everybody laughed.
"Willy's crying 'wolf' again," they said.

At last the wolf caught up with Willy.
"You shouldn't have told so many lies!" said
the grown-ups sternly.

The wolf heard the grown-ups and changed
his mind about eating Willy.

He ate the grown-ups instead.

Then...

he changed his mind again and had Willy for dessert.

C'est la vie.